MUSTACHE BABY

MEETS HIS MATCH

BRIDGET HEOS   ILLUSTRATIONS BY **JOY ANG**

CLARION BOOKS   Houghton Mifflin Harcourt
Boston   New York

CLARION BOOKS
215 Park Avenue South
New York, New York 10003

Clarion Books is an imprint of Houghton Mifflin Harcourt
Publishing Company

www.hmhco.com

The text was set in Tweed SG.
The illustrations in this book were executed digitally.

Library of Congress Cataloging-in-Publication Data is available.
ISBN 978-0-544-36375-5

Manufactured in China
SCP 10 9 8 7 6 5 4 3 2 1
4500506601

3200/4382

To Johnny, Richie, J.J., and Sami Jeanne
—B.H.

To my amazing parents, Jonna & Isidro Ang
—J.A.

Baby Billy was born with a mustache.
Usually it was a good-guy mustache,
but occasionally it curled up at the ends
into a—well, you know. Good mustache or bad,
Billy's family loved him.

Then one day,
Baby Javier came to town.
He was new and had a lot
to learn, so Billy decided to
show him a thing or two.

Like how he was the
sharpest shooter in the West.

And how he could work on
the railroad all the livelong day.

Javier couldn't believe how rough and tough Billy was.

But this wasn't Javier's first rodeo.
He had a few things of his own to show Billy.

Like how he could wrassle a bear.

Catch a fish with his bare hands.

And chop down a tree in no time flat.

Billy had never seen such grit. Except when he was looking in the mirror. He intended to prove that he was the true hero, and Javier was just his sidekick.

He challenged Javier to a duel.

But Javier disarmed Billy. . .

...and forced him to walk
the plank.

Then Billy put on a magic show and turned one cookie into two.

But Javier made both cookies disappear.

Billy tried to best Javier at:
Math.

Art.

Aviation.

Running for president.

And for the final showdown: A motorcycle race.

As they rounded the curve,

Billy was ahead by a hair. . .

But Javier won by a whisker.

That really chapped Billy's hide.
His mustache began to grow and curl
up at the ends until he had a . . .

BAD-GUY MUSTACHE.

He turned into a mad bandit, robbing Javier
of his most prized possession.

That infuriated Javier. Nobody stole his hog and got away with it. His beard grew pointier and pointier, until he had a . . .

Bad-Guy Beard.

Javier chased Billy into a wrestling ring and became
the masked *luchador* Barba Niño, AKA . . . Beard Baby!

Billy faced him as pro wrestler Mustache Baby.